D0811175

A SIENA BOOK

Siena is an imprint of Parragon Books
Published by Parragon Book Service Ltd,
Units 13 - 17, Avonbridge Trading Estate,
Atlantic Road, Avonmouth, Bristol BS11 9QD

Original concept by Julian Tucki • Improved by Guy Parr
Developed by Caroline Repchuk and Dug Steer

Produced by The Templar Company plc,
Pippbrook Mill, London Road, Dorking, Surrey RH4 1JE

Copyright © 1996 Parragon Book Service Ltd

Reprinted in 1998

Edited by Caroline Repchuk
Designed by Janie Louise Hunt

Printed and bound in Italy

ISBN 0-75251-328-1

THE
Jam Panda
Picnic

ILLUSTRATED BY STEPHANIE BOEY

WRITTEN BY DUGALD STEER

SIENA

One fine spring morning Peaches and Plum, the cheeky twins, woke up early and hurried downstairs. They were excited, because today the Jam Pandas were having their annual picnic in Bluebell Wood.

They helped Grandma pack the picnic basket full of lovely things to eat. There were sandwiches spread with all kinds of delicious jams. There was plum jam for Plum, and peach jam for Peaches. There were jam tarts, jam sponges and best of all, jam doughnuts!

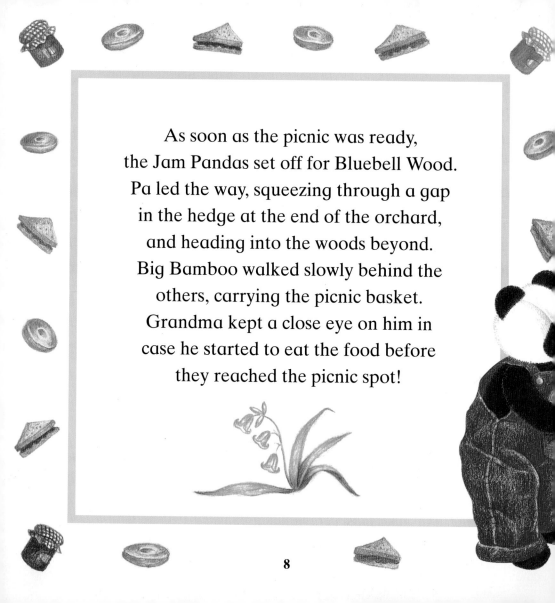

As soon as the picnic was ready,
the Jam Pandas set off for Bluebell Wood.
Pa led the way, squeezing through a gap
in the hedge at the end of the orchard,
and heading into the woods beyond.
Big Bamboo walked slowly behind the
others, carrying the picnic basket.
Grandma kept a close eye on him in
case he started to eat the food before
they reached the picnic spot!

Before long the Jam Pandas came to a clearing, where they stopped and spread out their blanket. Springtime was the very best time of the year in Bluebell Wood, with bluebells covering the ground in a thick carpet of blue. "Take care not to tread on the flowers!" said Pa.

As it was too early for lunch, Peaches and Plum decided to go and play hide and seek. "Come on Big Bamboo!" shouted Peaches. But Big Bamboo was almost asleep already. "Umph!" he said. "Wake me up when it's time for lunch."

The Jam Panda twins ran into the wood. They stopped by a big tree, and started their game. Plum covered his eyes and started counting up to twenty while Peaches ran off to hide.

13

Peaches soon found a good hiding place
in a big, twisted old oak tree which was
hollow inside. It was perfect!
From her hiding place she could
hear Plum, who was still counting.
"...eighteen, nineteen, twenty. I'm coming!"
he called.

Peaches didn't think it would take
Plum long to find her. She waited and waited.
But Plum didn't come. After a while, she
called out, "Plum, I'm here!"
But Plum still didn't come.

Peaches decided that she had waited long
enough. She didn't want to miss lunch!
She crawled out of her hiding place
and set off back to the picnic.

But poor Peaches couldn't fine her way back! She walked on and on through Bluebell Wood. "Ma!" she cried. "Pa! Grandma!" But nobody answered. Peaches was well and truly lost. She sat down on a tree stump and started to cry.

Meanwhile, Plum had been searching high
and low for Peaches but he just couldn't find
her. He started to get really worried, and
after looking everywhere he could think of,
he returned to the other pandas and told
them that Peaches had gone missing.

"Don't worry, Plum," said Grandma,
who had been unpacking the picnic.
"We will *all* look for Peaches!"

The Jam Pandas searched
all through the wood, but
there was no sign of Peaches.
Just then, as Ma was getting
really worried, she spotted a
trail of broken bluebells,
leading into the wood.
"Jumping Jamspoons!" said
Pa. "Peaches must have
forgotten not to tread on the
bluebells. We can follow her
trail!"

In no time at all, the trail led the Jam Pandas to Peaches. She was curled up fast asleep under a beech tree. Plum woke her up with a big hug. They were very glad to see each other!

Just then, Big Bamboo's tummy rumbled and everyone laughed. "I think it's picnic time," said Grandma.

Back at the picnic spot they were all soon tucking into a delicious jammy feast. Big Bamboo insisted he needed an extra large helping of blackcurrant jam to restore his energy levels after the search, and Ma made sure Peaches got a specially big helping of her favourite peach jam. "At least one thing is certain," chuckled Pa, biting into a big jammy doughnut. "When it comes to picnics, Grandma always makes sure *nothing* is missing!"

27

• T H E   E N D •